D1195329

For Jana, Ashoka, Simon, Kai, and Han

Bala Kids
An imprint of Shambhala Publications, Inc.
4720 Walnut Street
Boulder, Colorado 80301
www.shambhala.com

Text © 2021 by Maya van der Meer
Illustrations © 2021 by Wen Hsu-Chen

All rights reserved. No part of this book may be reproduced in any form or by any means, electronic or mechanical, including photocopying, recording, or by any information storage and retrieval system, without permission in writing from the publisher.

9 8 7 6 5 4 3 2 1

First Edition
Printed in China

♾This edition is printed on acid-free paper that meets the American National Standards Institute Z39.48 Standard.
♻Shambhala Publications makes every effort to print on recycled paper.
For more information please visit www.shambhala.com.
Bala Kids is distributed worldwide by Penguin Random House, Inc., and its subsidiaries.

Designed by Kara Plikaitis

Library of Congress Cataloging-in-Publication Data
Names: Meer, Maya van der, author. | Hsu, Wen, 1976– illustrator.
Title: Kuan Yin: the princess who became the Goddess of Compassion / Maya van der Meer;
illustrated by Wen Hsu.
Description: Boulder, Colorado: Bala Kids, 2021. | Audience: Ages 4–8 |
Audience: Grades K–1
Identifiers: LCCN 2019034968 | ISBN 9781611807998 (hardcover)
Subjects: LCSH: Avalokiteśvara (Buddhist deity)—Juvenile literature.
Classification: LCC BQ4710.A8 M44 2021 | DDC 294.3/4211—dc23
LC record available at https://lccn.loc.gov/2019034968

KUAN YIN

THE PRINCESS WHO BECAME THE
GODDESS OF COMPASSION

Maya van der Meer | Illustrated by Wen Hsu

bala kids

Williamsburg Regional Library
757-741-3300   www.wrl.org
OCT - - 2021

Every morning, Princess Ling awoke to find her big sister sitting at the foot of her bed. Princess Miao Shan always sat very still with a gentle smile on her lips. Ling would watch the slight movements of her sister's silk robes as she breathed deeply and steadily in meditation.

Miao Shan's calming presence filled the room
with the sweet scent of a lotus flower.

But on this morning, Ling awoke with a start to the
creaking of the wooden screens on her bedroom window.
She opened her eyes and caught sight of the ends of
Miao Shan's robes slipping off the windowsill.
"Wait!" Ling cried as she jumped to the floor.
She reached the window just in time to see Miao Shan
disappear into the dense forest surrounding the palace.

As she arrived to the dining hall, Ling caught sight of a long line of princes eagerly waiting, each holding rare and expensive gifts in the hopes of winning the famous Princess Miao Shan's hand in marriage. Ling suddenly understood the reason for her sister's disappearance.

"Where is your sister?!" the king boomed at Ling as she arrived for breakfast alone. Ling trembled beneath the fierce gaze of her father's black eyes. She knew if she told the truth, her sister would be punished.

"Maybe . . . she's at the fish pond," Ling replied meekly.

"That girl prefers feeding fish over fulfilling her duty to her own family," the king grumbled under his breath. Red in the face, he turned to the servants. "Go find her now!" he commanded, slamming his fist on the table.

After breakfast, Ling raced to her room. Her lie would send the king's search party to the fish pond first, but it wouldn't buy her much time. She tucked a napkin with a little food from breakfast into a leather pouch and quickly slipped through the open window.

As she ventured out to find her sister, Ling's head was spinning with worry. Her delicate skirts caught on brambles in the thick undergrowth, and a wave of fear passed through her. Just then, she smelled the familiar fragrance of a lotus flower. Turning in the direction of the scent, she spotted her sister beneath the dappled shade of a willow tree.

Ling rubbed her eyes in disbelief. There sat Princess Miao Shan, relaxed and natural, surrounded by a group of wild animals lying calmly at her feet. A faint orb of light encircled them all. Miao Shan looked up from her meditation and smiled, motioning for Ling to come closer.

Relieved to find her sister, Ling stepped into the light. A great tigress napped like a kitten. A wild boar rested his tusks between outstretched hooves. With no sign of worry, birds, mice, butterflies, and beetles relaxed alongside a huge hawk, a family of foxes, the boar, and the tigress. Miao Shan then made a gentle gesture to bid her animal friends farewell. They roused slowly, and the moment they stepped outside the circle of light, they raced into the forest, wild again. As the last animal left, the light surrounding Ling and Miao Shan dissolved.

"It's so good to see you, little sister!" Miao Shan said, hugging Ling tightly. "It pained me to leave without saying goodbye this morning."

"How is all this possible?" Ling marveled.

Princess Miao Shan took Ling's small hand. "It is all possible by the power of love, my dear sister," she said with a wink. "I have a lot to share with you, but we have all day."

"No, we don't!" Ling suddenly remembered. "Our father has sent a search party, and they will soon find us and punish you!"

"Yes, Father will punish me for refusing to marry," Miao Shan replied. "He doesn't accept that I've chosen to follow a spiritual path rather than a worldly one, that I would rather ease the pain of others than rule over them. But don't worry, Ling. I promise, even if I have to go away, you will find me when it's time. Just like you did today."

Ling settled a bit, trusting Miao Shan.

By nightfall, all the disappointed
princes had left the palace, and
the search party came back to
the court empty-handed. Furious,
the king barely noticed when
Miao Shan silently appeared in
the doorway. Ling cowered
behind her sister as the
king scolded Miao Shan.

"How dare you betray
me and risk the future of
my reign!" he yelled.

"Father, I'm sorry you are upset, but I have decided to follow a different path. Please, let me go to White Sparrow Nunnery so I can train myself to be of true service to all beings," Miao Shan pleaded. "This will benefit our kingdom and family far more than if I marry."

The king pressed his eyebrows together and thought: *I will send my ungrateful daughter to the nunnery, but I will command the nuns to make her life miserable with impossible tasks. She will quickly tire of such a life and return to the palace.*

They followed the king's orders and did not allow Miao Shan to become a nun. She instead only received grueling work to fill her days. When Ling visited her sister at the nunnery, she found her worn and disheveled, plowing a barren field that hadn't grown a single blade of grass in over fifty years.

"Sister, nothing can grow here! Why don't you just give up and come home?" Ling paused for a moment to let her true feelings come through. "I miss you so much, Miao Shan," she said and began to cry.

Miao Shan pushed back her knotted hair and knelt down. "Let's make a wish, not just for ourselves, but for all beings: may the seeds we plant with our hearts grow." She guided Ling's hand to touch the ground. Ling concentrated all the energy of her heart into the soil. She wished for all beings, including her sister, to be happy and at ease.

Suddenly, lightning flashed over the field. Ling opened her eyes and saw a golden dragon swooping down. In one swift motion of his gigantic tail, the dragon made a deep pool of water for Miao Shan to irrigate the field.

Then, a great cloud gathered on the horizon, rapidly approaching. As it drew near, Ling realized it was flocks of birds, carrying seeds in their beaks. They landed all around and began planting.

"Look, Ling." Miao Shan smiled with relief. "Your heartfelt wish worked. Thank you."

Miao Shan eventually coaxed every inch of that field back to life. She grew food to feed the poor and herbs to make medicines for the sick. Ling spent hours in the lush greenery talking with Miao Shan as they gardened. They spoke about the importance of caring for every living being equally, from a tiny earthworm to a powerful king like their father.

As the days passed, the seeds that were planted with love grew and spread happiness.

Flowers bloomed everywhere. Children came to play and pick blossoms for their mothers. Their laughter filled the perfumed air. The people were happy. The animals were happy. The sisters were happy. Everyone was happy. Everyone, that is, except the king.

When the king learned of Miao Shan's accomplishments, he flew into a rage and stormed off to the nunnery.

Seeing their father, Ling was terrified he would take Miao Shan away forever. "Please, Father, let Miao Shan be! She is doing good things." The king ignored Ling and raced toward Miao Shan.

A powerful growl echoed through the garden, and a great tigress, the very same one Ling had seen resting at Miao Shan's feet in the forest, bounded in out of nowhere and stood between the king and his daughter.

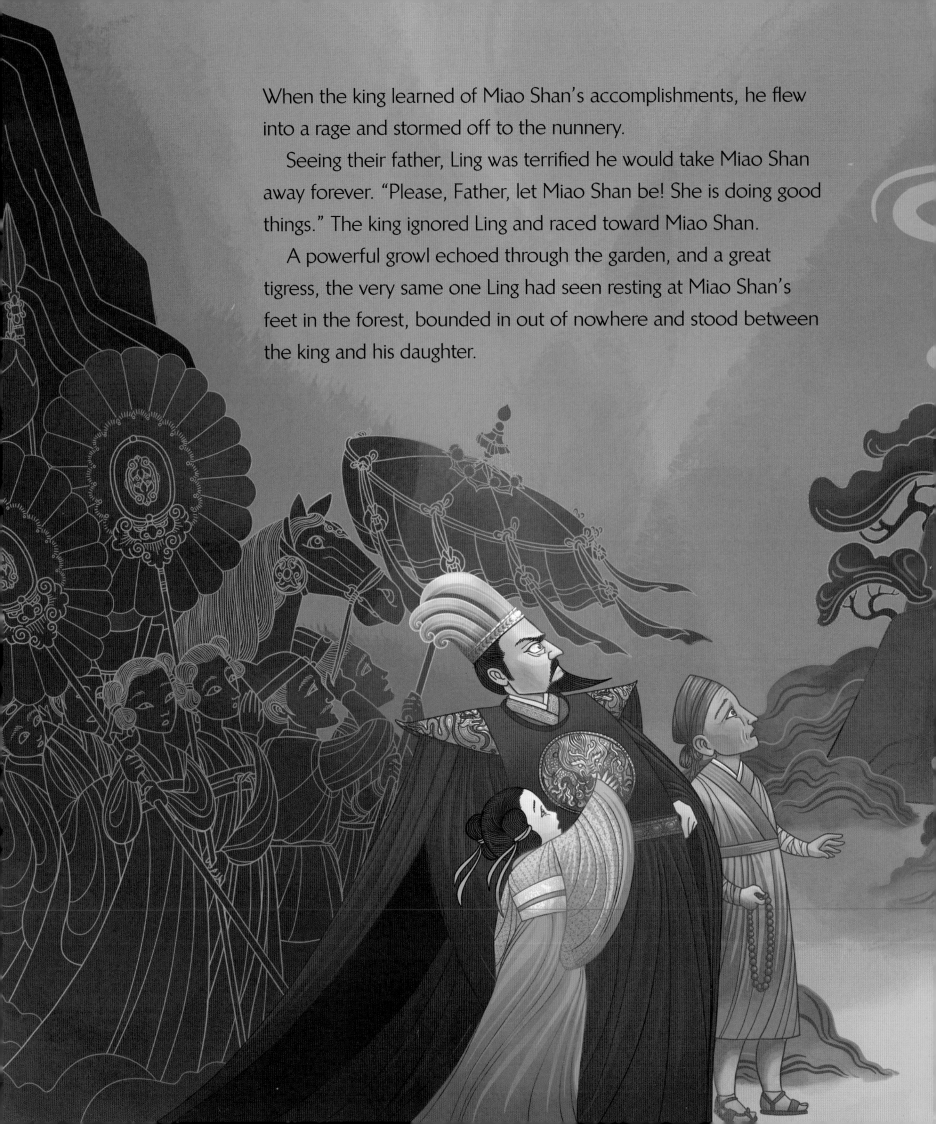

Miao Shan gave Ling a gentle smile, then quickly straddled her trusted friend. The two leapt off, vanishing into a mysterious mist that had descended over the garden.

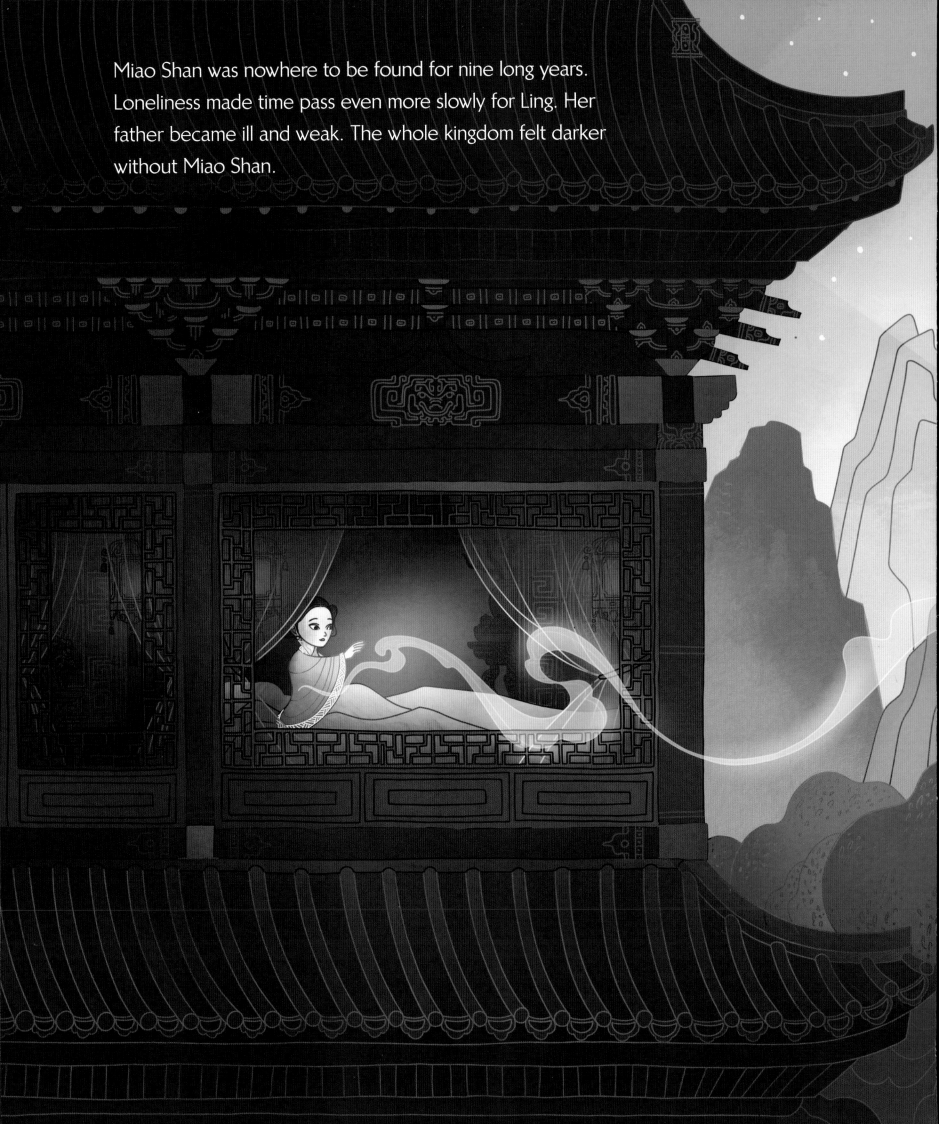

Miao Shan was nowhere to be found for nine long years.
Loneliness made time pass even more slowly for Ling. Her
father became ill and weak. The whole kingdom felt darker
without Miao Shan.

Finally, one spring morning, the fragrance of Miao Shan's presence filled Ling's room again. "It's just a dream," Ling said to herself, burrowing into the silken covers. But the scent soon overpowered her sleep. She sat up, certain her sister must be somewhere near. Excitedly, Ling dressed and slipped

The perfume led Ling to Fragrant Mountain, the place where the tigress had taken Princess Miao Shan and where she had remained in deep meditation ever since. As Ling arrived, petals rained down. Rainbows shone everywhere. The fragrance was so strong, it made her think, *All the flowers in the world must live on this one mountain.*

Finally, Ling found her sister sitting atop a giant lotus flower, as if on a throne, radiating a soothing light. In that moment, Ling knew Miao Shan had fully realized the power of love. She raced into her sister's arms and all her sadness and fear melted away.

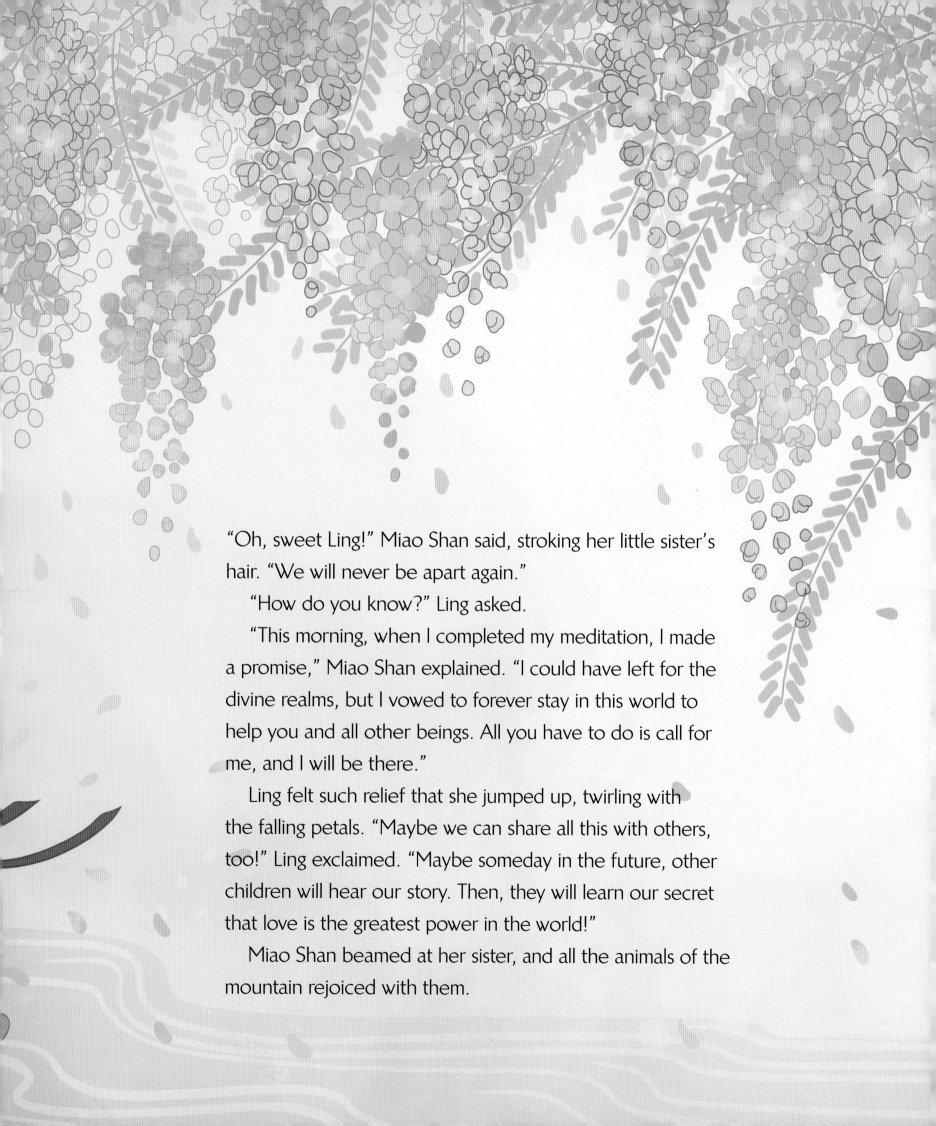

"Oh, sweet Ling!" Miao Shan said, stroking her little sister's hair. "We will never be apart again."

"How do you know?" Ling asked.

"This morning, when I completed my meditation, I made a promise," Miao Shan explained. "I could have left for the divine realms, but I vowed to forever stay in this world to help you and all other beings. All you have to do is call for me, and I will be there."

Ling felt such relief that she jumped up, twirling with the falling petals. "Maybe we can share all this with others, too!" Ling exclaimed. "Maybe someday in the future, other children will hear our story. Then, they will learn our secret that love is the greatest power in the world!"

Miao Shan beamed at her sister, and all the animals of the mountain rejoiced with them.

Suddenly, Ling heard the voice of their father and froze.

"Miao Shan? Is that really you?" the king asked in disbelief. "Are you the wise healer I have come to thank for saving my life?"

"Yes, Father. I heard you were sick, so I sent medicines. I am relieved to see they helped."

The king dropped to his knees before Miao Shan. "I have been so cruel to you, yet you saved my life."

Miao Shan placed her hand gently on her father's massive shoulder. The king began to cry. "Please forgive me, precious daughter. How can I ever repay your kindness?"

"All I ask is that you devote the rest of your life to ruling your kingdom with kindness," Miao Shan replied.

So it came to pass that this once terrifying king became a good and just ruler. With his newfound power of love, he built a beautiful temple on Fragrant Mountain for his daughter, and happiness in the kingdom spread far and wide.

This is how Princess Miao Shan became the immortal Kuan Yin, the one who hears the cries of the world. To this day, millions of people call on her when love and compassion are needed. They visit her temples and say her name with their prayers. You can, too. If you feel frightened or need to find light in the darkness of any difficulty you are facing, the power of Kuan Yin's love can be awakened in your heart. Simply think of her and remember this story.

Author's Note

Kuan Yin is perhaps the most widely revered Buddhist saint in the world. Known as Avalokiteshvara in Sanskrit, Kannon in Japanese, and Chenrezig in Tibetan, this bodhisattva of compassion is at the heart of all Mahayana Buddhist traditions. Kuan Yin, who is sometimes depicted as male and other times as female, took the vow to free all sentient beings from their suffering.

The legend of Miao Shan is a traditional Chinese origin story of Kuan Yin. Miao Shan was a princess who lived in a country called Raised Forest thousands of years ago. Instead of marrying a prince according to her father's wishes, she followed her own path of spiritual practice and left the royal life behind. This was unheard of in her traditional culture, where family roles were viewed as the foundation of society. The artwork is inspired by the Tang Dynasty and depicts clothing styles from across the Silk Road.

This modern telling follows Ling, Miao Shan's younger sister, who witnesses her sister's trials, perseverance, and ultimate enlightenment. Ling must overcome doubts, fears, and loneliness in order to realize what her sister tells her all along: that love, which is ultimately compassion for others, is the greatest power in the world.